Merri-Lee Monarch

HAPPY READING!

This book is especially for:

Suzanne Tate
Author—
brings fun and
facts to us in her
Nature Series.

James Melvin
Illustrator—
brings joyous life
to Suzanne
Tate's
characters.

Author Suzanne Tate
and
Illustrator James Melvin

Merri-Lee Monarch

A Tale of a Big Trip
Suzanne Tate
Illustrated by James Melvin

Nags Head Art

To Emily
caring and
loving Mema

ISBN 978-1-878405-65-4

Published by
Nags Head Art, Inc., P.O. Box 2149, Manteo, NC 27954
Copyright © 2018 by Suzanne Tate
First Edition

Merri-Lee Monarch was a pretty butterfly. Her wings were brightly colored in orange and black.

Merri-Lee flew merrily all day long. She liked to fly around in a garden that was full of flowers.

Many monarchs were there.
The butterflies could get food
they needed from the flowers.

Merri-Lee's brother, Monty Monarch,
was in the garden, too.

"You should slow down and stop to feed,"
Monty said to Merri-Lee.

"We need to store lots of food
in our bodies."

He landed on a flower and began
to slurp up sweet nectar from it.

"Well, if you say so, I will stop to sip,"
Merri-Lee said, as she chose a flower.

"HELPFUL HUMANS have planted milkweed and flowers in the garden for us," Monty said.

Merri-Lee exclaimed, "I am thankful for HELPFUL HUMANS!"

About that time, she saw a caterpillar feeding on a milkweed plant.

"Ewwww! What is that scary thing?" Merri-Lee cried.

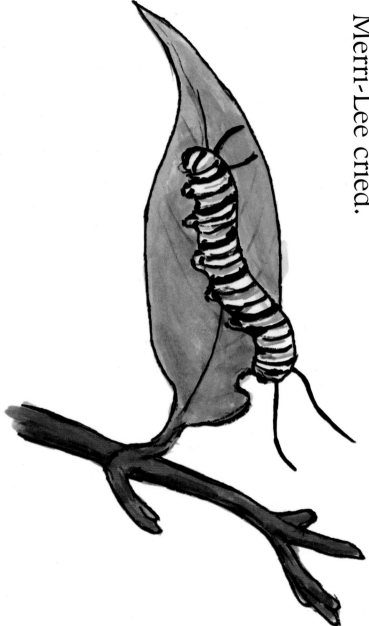

"That is a monarch caterpillar. You once looked like that!" Monty replied.

"The plant it is eating has bitter juices.
When it becomes a butterfly like you,
hungry birds stay away!"

"They know a monarch tastes bad."

But Merri-Lee wondered how she ever changed from a caterpillar to a butterfly.

She asked Monty if he could tell her.

"Oh, yes, that is another interesting story," Monty said. "A monarch caterpillar hatches from a tiny egg. Then, it eats a lot of milkweed."

Egg

"It becomes fat and splits its old skin four times in order to grow larger."

"Then, the caterpillar finds a place to attach itself,"
Monty said, "and begins to change!
The caterpillar's skin splits one more time."

Caterpillar   Skin Splits   Chrysalis

"A soft shell has formed under its skin.
Then, the shell is called a chrysalis."

"The chrysalis turns hard to protect itself," Monty continued. "In about one week, it cracks open."

Turns hard

Cracks open

Butterfly!

"Suddenly, a butterfly emerges just like you and I!" Monty said.

Merri-Lee was amazed to hear how she
was once a caterpillar – and then,
a beautiful butterfly!

But the most *amazing* part of the monarch story
was about to begin for Merri-Lee and Monty.

It was the true tale of a

BIG GRUB.

Days in the garden became shorter.
"Something is telling me to fly south,"
Merri-Lee said.

"Yes," Monty agreed.
"We must fly to a new place.
It will be fun – a Big Trip!"

Merri-Lee and Monty left the garden. They began to fly south with many other monarch butterflies.

All the monarchs were drawn like a magnet to a faraway place.

But it was a dangerous trip!
They had to fly thousands of miles to
reach their winter home in Mexico.

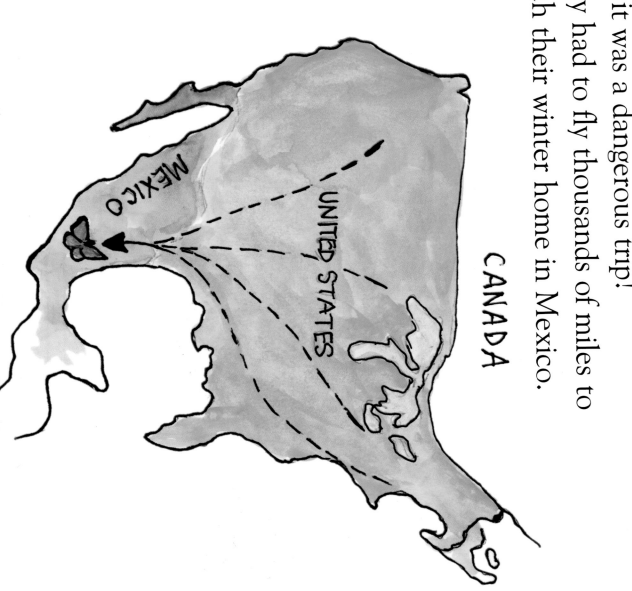

Hungry animals – like lizards and toads
– grabbed them when they stopped to rest.
And if the wind blew strong, the butterflies
could be swept to sea.

The butterflies stopped to sip some nectar along the way. It made them strong and helped them in their Big Trip.

After flying on and on, Merri-Lee sighed,
"I am so tired." Monty was tired, too.
"We must stop a little while," he said.

They joined other monarchs
that were hanging on a tree to rest.

Merri-Lee and Monty and millions
of monarchs flew until they reached
a special forest in Mexico.

The butterflies came together in clusters on fir trees. They stayed there all winter and didn't eat!

When the weather turned warm,
the monarchs became active.

They quickly flew about, choosing mates.

Then, the butterflies knew to fly north.

Merri-Lee and other females stopped often to lay eggs on leaves of milkweed.

At last, Merri-Lee arrived at a garden where HELPFUL HUMANS had planted milkweed and flowers.

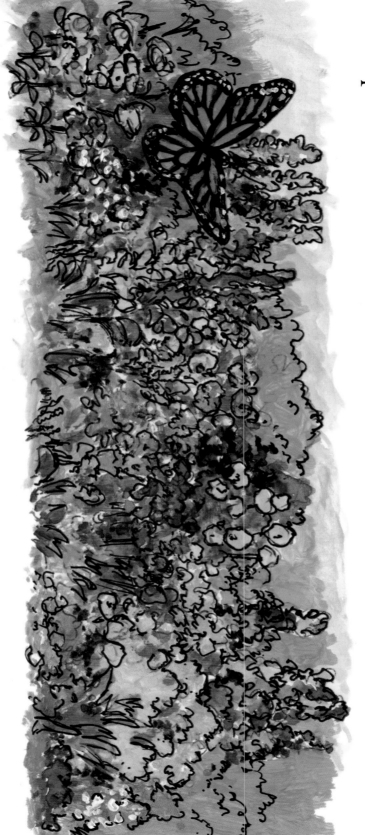

Merri-Lee was happy to be there.

"Monty was right," she thought.

"It was a really Big Trip!"